this book belongs to:

The Magician

Story by Sherri Maret

Illustrations by Pamela Behrend

THE RoadRunner Press

Oklahoma City, Oklahoma

From the author
To Tim, Michael, Whitney, Charla, and Holly.
Your love and support have been magical!

From the illustrator
Dedicated with love to the ones who bring
just the right amount of chaos and inspiration to my life:
Ken, Kenny, James, Abby, Max, and the Piggies

Holly Foster tapped the black top hat three times, reached deep inside, and pulled out . . .

"A bunny!" the children shouted with glee.

"I would like to introduce you to Mr. Buddy the Bunny," said Holly, holding the chubby rabbit high in the air so all could see.

"Awww, he is so cute!" a little girl cried.

Buddy gave her a big wink.

"The bunny is real!" a boy exclaimed.

"How did you do that, Miss Holly?" another little boy asked.

"Magic," Holly said with a little bow.

The children clapped and begged for more. Holly happily obliged.

After the show, Holly packed up her gear. As she gently stowed away her top hat, she confided to Buddy, "I wish we could do this every day."

Buddy agreed
in his rabbity way.
Quietly.

Holly, you see, loved magic.

She came by that love from her favorite uncle, a magician who began teaching her magic tricks when Holly was still just a little girl.

At school when classmates talked about growing up to be a firefighter or a teacher or a doctor, Holly's answer was always the same: "I am going to be a magician just like my Uncle Bob."

"A magician!" a boy in her class sputtered. "Impossible! You are a girl. Everyone knows that girls can only be a magician's assistant."

"Nope! I am going to be a magician," Holly replied as she pulled a coin out of the boy's ear.

On her tenth birthday, Uncle Bob gave Holly a bunny, her first live prop.

"Every magician needs a rabbit," her uncle said.

"Thank you!" said Holly. "I will name him Buddy."

When Holly joined the Society of Young Magicians, Buddy could not help but notice she did not look like any of the other magicians.

Holly and Buddy began to perform magic for children at libraries, schools, and birthday parties whenever they could. Buddy wanted to help Holly realize her dream of being a professional magician. He was good at being pulled out of a hat. Was it possible he could do more for his friend?

He set out to try.

Buddy quickly discovered that doing magic without Holly did not always go as planned.

"Have you been like that all day?" asked Holly, unlocking the trick handcuffs.

Buddy nodded
in his rabbity way.
Quietly.

Then one day an old trunk arrived at Holly's door, with a note.

Dear Holly,

I have performed my final show—my last

Indian Rope Trick left me disappeared for too long.

I pass my wand to you.

Your loving uncle,

The Remarkable Roberto!

(Uncle Bob)

The old trunk was filled with magic books and props galore!

"Maybe the secret to becoming a magician like Uncle Bob is in one of these old magic books," Holly whispered.

Buddy overheard her
and wished
the same in his
rabbity way.
Quietly.

When Holly left for work the next day, Buddy was already reading one of the big magic books.

Buddy read magic books all morning. Buddy read magic books all afternoon. Buddy was still reading a magic book long after Holly had returned from her job and gone off to bed.

The clock had just struck midnight when it happened.

Aha! Buddy said to himself
in his rabbity way.
Quietly.

The next morning, Holly found Buddy sketching so furiously she slipped out the front door for work without saying a word so as not to bother him.

She could not help but wonder what Buddy was up to.

Meanwhile, Buddy had run into a glitch.

As he pondered the problem, it suddenly occured to him—maybe a neighbor could help!

Before you could say *abracadabra*, out the window he went!

It took a few weeks for Holly to add the beautiful and many more for Holly and Buddy to master the illusion. Finally it was time to share their magic with the world.

Holly signed them up for "Night of the New Magicians."

Holly and Buddy were both excited and a little nervous about their performance because the biggest stars from the Society of Magicians would be in the audience.

On the night of their debut, magicians from around the world and people both young and old streamed into the theater.

Holly and Buddy opened with a few of their more conventional magic tricks.

Then Holly stepped forward.

"Ladies and gentlemen," she announced, "we would like to close our performance tonight with our newest illusion. We call it, 'A Bed of Roses.' "

Without another word from Holly, a bed covered in flowers rolled onto the stage.

Holly took her place on the rose-covered bed.

Buddy covered her with a blue drape from head to toe.

Holly took a deep breath. For the magic to work, she had to remain as still as a statue.

Buddy waved his wand.

The crowd gasped as the bed, with Holly on it, began to rise.

Buddy tapped the stage with his wand. The bed began to descend slowly. When it was within Buddy's reach, he waved his wand and whipped the blue drape off and away.

Holly was gone! The roses were gone, too!

In their place were white doves, which took flight, soaring up, up, and away.

The audience sat stunned. A murmur began to spread. "Where did she go? Where did she go?"

Buddy tapped his wand once more and pointed to a theatre box high above the crowd.

All heads turned and looked up.

Holly, dressed in black
feathers with a beak,
perched on the balcony
like a majestic bird.

"Ooooh!" said the crowd.

Holly stood and curtsied.

She raised her enormous wings and . . . took flight.

"Ahhhh!" said the crowd.

Holly glided to the stage and landed softly next to Buddy as the audience burst into thunderous applause and rose as one in a standing ovation.

Holly took a bow, and so did Buddy.

"We did it, Buddy! We made our dream come true," Holly said.

She gave Buddy a big hug and then whispered, "Do you think we could come up with another grand illusion?"

Buddy nodded
in his rabbity way.
Quietly.

The End

Magic

noun: the art of producing illusions by sleight of hand
adjective: giving a feeling of enchantment
verb: to produce, remove, or influence by magic

1. The word *magic* comes from the Greek word *magikē*; akin to the ancient Persian *magus* for sorcerer.

2. Performing magic became a respectable profession only in the early eighteenth century. Before that, it was limited to jugglers and sword swallowers at fairs and circuses.

3. The distinctive top hat and tailcoat of the magician can be traced to Alexander Herrmann, a French magician known as Herrmann the Great. After Herrmann, people expected magicians to be so dressed.

4. The largest magic organization is the International Brotherhood of Magicians, but the oldest is the Society of American Magicians, established May 10, 1902, in New York City with twenty-four members.

5. In July 1984, The Society of Young Magicians was founded. Learn more at www.MagicSAM.com!

Making Magic

The secret to making magic is to start with simple magic tricks, and then practice, practice, practice! Here are some of my favorite books on the subject:

Big Magic for Little Hands: 25 Astounding Illusions for Young Magicians by Joshua Jay

101 Ways to Amaze & Entertain:
Amazing Magic & Hilarious Jokes To Try on Your Friends & Family by Peter Gross

Children's Book of Magic by DK Publishing

Abracadabra!: Fun Magic Tricks for Kids by Kristen Kelly, Ken Kelly, and Colette Kelly

The Usborne Complete Book of Magic by Cheryl Evans and Ian Keable-Elliott.